Bialosky
and the Big Parade Mystery

By Justine Korman • Illustrated by Tom Cooke

Created by Peggy & Alan Bialosky

A GOLDEN BOOK · NEW YORK

Western Publishing Company, Inc., Racine, Wisconsin 53404

Bialosky loved the Independence Day Parade. Even if the fireworks fizzled as they did last year, there were always plenty of Mrs. Elvira B. Buzz's honey nut muffins to eat.

This year the parade was going to be even better, because Bialosky was in the trumpet corps of the marching band.

"It's time to practice," said Bialosky on the morning of July Fourth. He searched around for his trumpet. "Oh, bumblebees! I can't find it!"

Just then Bialosky heard footsteps outside.

"I hope it's Brownie," he thought. "He'll help me find my trumpet."

Bialosky opened the door and saw a tall, thin man. He wore a dark suit and carried a metal suitcase with a big lock on it.

"He's a mighty strange-looking stranger," thought Bialosky.

Moments later Brownie arrived. He'd seen the stranger, too.

"I wonder what he's doing in our little town," said Brownie.

"There's plenty to wonder about," Bialosky said. "I can't find my trumpet."

"We have to find it," Brownie said. "You can't march without it!"

Bialosky had been looking forward to wearing his tall, fancy band hat, but he put on his detective hat instead. It was time to solve a mystery.

Brownie was looking out the window. "The stranger's heading downtown," he said.

"Aha!" declared Bialosky. "Let's follow him."

"What about your trumpet?" asked Brownie.

"One mystery at a time," said Bialosky.

So the bears followed the stranger.

"I've never seen a suitcase like that before,"
Brownie remarked.

"Highly suspicious," said Bialosky.

They watched the stranger walk up the steps of
Town Hall.

"Maybe he's going to see the mayor," said
Brownie.

Bialosky nodded. "I'm sure we're on to
something big."

Sure enough, the stranger came out of Town Hall with Mayor Munch. Bialosky and Brownie followed them across the square to the Park Hotel.

On the way, the two bears met their friend Suzie.
They told her about the stranger, and then they all went into
the hotel.

By now, Suzie was suspicious, too. "That's odd,"
she said. "The stranger brought his suitcase into the
dining room. Most people leave their suitcases and packages
in the checkroom."

"We've got to find out what's going on," Bialosky said excitedly.

"Let's disguise ourselves as waiters," Suzie suggested. "Then we can listen in on the mayor and the stranger."

Bialosky wasted no time. He spotted a laundry cart full of waiters' jackets and he grabbed three.

"What should we do now?" asked Brownie, rolling up the sleeves of his jacket.

"Watch the other waiters," said Suzie. "Act like them."

"And be on the lookout for clues," added Bialosky, reluctantly removing his detective hat.

Suzie slipped in front of the busy waiter who was serving the mayor's table.

"I'll help you with that," she said, taking the water pitcher from him.

She listened closely while she poured the water, but the mayor and the stranger were talking only about the menu.

CAUTION
HANDLE WITH

Suzie hurried back to her friends.

"The label on the suitcase says 'Caution, Handle with Care,'" she reported.

"That suitcase gets more suspicious by the minute," Bialosky declared.

Meanwhile, Brownie served rolls and butter.

Seconds later Brownie returned.

"They were talking about explosives," he said.

"Not about the salmon?" Suzie asked.

"There's something fishy about this case," said
Bialosky, and he rushed off to the mayor's table.

The mayor was saying, "It's almost time for the parade."

Just then, the real waiter handed Bialosky a tray full of dirty dishes.

"Take these to the kitchen right away," the waiter said.

Bialosky hurried off.

"We've got to go," Bialosky told his friends.
"The parade is about to start!"

"But we still don't know where your trumpet is,"
Brownie said.

"Your trumpet?" asked Suzie.

In all the excitement about the stranger, Bialosky
had forgotten to tell Suzie about the missing trumpet.

"I know," said Suzie. "You can take my flute. I'll run home and get it."

"But I don't know how to play it," said Bialosky.

"You can pretend," Brownie said. "At least you'll get to wear your uniform and march."

The thought of his uniform and his hat made Bialosky feel better. "Okay, Suzie," he said. "We'll meet you at the parade."

Back home, Bialosky changed into his uniform.
"What a handsome uniform," Brownie exclaimed.
"What a handsome bear," Bialosky added, admiring
himself. "And now for the crowning touch…"

When Bialosky lifted his band hat, he couldn't believe
his eyes. There was his trumpet!
He laughed, and Brownie joined in.
"It must have been there all the time," said Bialosky.

At the parade ground, Brownie told Suzie the good news about Bialosky's trumpet.

"Hurray!" Suzie cheered. "Here, Brownie, take my flute so you can march, too."

"Thanks!" Brownie said, and he rushed over to join Bialosky and the marching band.

It was a wonderful parade. Bialosky marched proudly
in his tall band hat. Brownie followed happily behind him.
And Suzie dropped her baton only once.

Later Mayor Munch made an announcement.

"Tonight's fireworks will be launched by a genuine expert from the big city," he said.

"The stranger!" Bialosky exclaimed. He felt just as he had when he'd lifted his band hat and found his trumpet.

"The fireworks must have been in his suitcase," Suzie concluded.

"Maybe next time we'll solve the case before it solves itself," Brownie teased.

Then, with a loud *crack*, the sky was filled with a colorful burst of fireworks.

"Oooh," said Suzie.

"Aaah," said Brownie.

"Aha!" said Bialosky.